I Think My Chicken Is a Dinosaur

BY KATHLEEN O'NEILL OSWALD
ILLUSTRATED BY ESTHER HERNANDO

Copyright © 2024 by Kathleen Oswald. All rights reserved. This book may not be reproduced or stored in whole or in part by any means without the written permission of the author except for brief quotations for the purpose of review.

ISBN: 978-1-960146-67-0 Hard cover
978-1-960146-68-7 Soft cover

Editing: Amy Ashby

Published by Warren Publishing
Charlotte, NC
www.warrenpublishing.net
Printed in the United States

For my three paleontologists:
Wyatt, Wesley, and Emmett

Deep in the jungle of sod and hay

lies a BEAST to be awakened at the CRACK of day.

A PREHISTORIC connection soon to appear,
a CREATURE in the making, 65 million years.

It may sound STRANGE, but wait to hear more ...

I think my CHICKEN

is a DINOSAUR!

CHICKENS and DINOS—flocks of a feather?

Can't handle the cold ... better knit him a sweater.
(Maybe a sweater of FEATHERS would work better!)

Scientists aren't sure about DINOSAUR sounds;
I bet they COOED and CLUCKED as they STOMPED on the ground.

And yes, they have WINGS, but chickens can't FLY;

like ARCHAEOPTERYXES, they spread their wings to GLIDE.

CHICKENS have bones that are hollow,

just like the RAPTORS before.

I think my CHICKEN is a DINOSAUR!

Still not convinced little PEEP is a scary FOWL?

Then you haven't met a ROOSTER out on the PROWL.

He stalks his prey on THREE-TOED FEET,

makes quick meals of GRAIN and each BUG he meets.

Instincts passed down with each GENERATION,

a rooster twenty feet tall would have a T-REX reputation.

And he'd claim his TERRITORY with a cock-a-doodle-ROAR!

So, don't you be fooled by the FLUFF and the FEATHERS; behind the CUTENESS is a DEADLY predator.

As a PALEONTOLOGIST, each day I complete my chores, knowing I am in the presence of DINOSAURS!

What Is a Theory?

A theory is a BIG IDEA that helps scientists explain how or why things happened. Theories are not facts but ideas that allow scientists to study and learn about things from long ago. It is a scientist's job to gather evidence, and sometimes they link those facts and create a theory about them.

I Think My Chicken Is a Dinosaur explores one of the most popular dinosaur theories—that some dinosaurs could have been related to birds!

The Evidence:
Not all dinosaurs fit our bird theory. The group of dinosaurs that are believed to be related to birds are called Theropods. This group of dinosaurs includes Tyrannosaurus rexes, Velociraptors, and Archaeopteryxes.

Feathers
Scientists believe that many dinosaurs were warm-blooded—just like birds! They also believe that some of our favorite dinosaurs were covered in feathers. These feathers would have been used to keep the animals warm and help regulate their temperature. So, just like our story suggests, our dino friends had sweaters made of feathers!

Fossils also show that dinosaurs like Velociraptors had bones with quill knobs on the ulna just like birds do. These quill knobs are bumps that anchor feathers. This is strong evidence that some of our favorite dinosaurs looked less like lizards and more like birds.

Hollow Bones
One of the strongest connections between birds and dinosaurs is that their bones are hollow. These bones allowed dinos to be lighter and faster and even allowed some to take flight. The dinosaur that is most closely related to birds is the Archaeopteryx, which spread its wings to glide. The bird that is most closely related to dinosaurs is the turkey, whose size and bone structure are very similar to a Velociraptor's.

Three-toed Feet
Birds and some dinosaurs (Theropods) have a very similar footprint—they all have three toes! But only recently do fossils show that dinosaurs, just like birds, also have a fourth toe that faces backwards. Birds use this toe to hold on to branches, defend themselves, and hunt. Dinosaurs like the T-rex would have used this toe's long talon to become fierce predators.

Egg Laying
Most scientists believe that dinosaurs laid eggs to reproduce. Fossils of eggs and nests have been found, and scientists have even discovered fossils of dinosaurs roosting or sleeping on nests exactly as birds would.

Bibliography

"How Dinosaurs Were Similar to Birds." *Creative Beast Studio*. April 26, 2021. https://creative-beast.com/how-dinosaurs-were-similar-to-birds/.

"It's Official: Birds Are Literally Dinosaurs. Here's How We Know." Bird Life International. December 21, 2021. https://www.birdlife.org/news/2021/12/21/its-official-birds-are-literally-dinosaurs-heres-how-we-know/#:~:text=The%20strong%20evidence%20doesn't, but%20distinctive%20bird%2Dlike%20feathers.

Fuller-Wright, Liz. "Dinosaur-Era Bird Tracks: Proof of 100-Million-Year-Old Flight?" *The Christian Science Monitor*. October 28, 2013. https://www.csmonitor.com/Science/2013/1028/Dinosaur-era-bird-tracks-Proof-of-100-million-year-old-flight.

Mancini, Mark. "Meet Archaeopteryx, a Feathered Dino with Wings and Teeth." *How Stuff Works*. December 29, 2020. https://animals.howstuffworks.com/dinosaurs/archaepteryx.htm.

Maxwell, Colby. "Turkey Vulture Size & Wingspan: Just How Big Are They?" *A-Z Animals*. February 3, 2022. https://a-z-animals.com/blog/turkey-vulture-size-wingspan-just-how-big-are-they/.

About the Author

Kathleen Oswald lives on a small farm in South Carolina with her husband Nathan and three boys. The family decided to expand the farm and adopted six baby chicks. As the chickens grew, the boys began to play with them and noticed the similarities to their favorite dinosaurs. The chicks soon were all named Rex and Blue, and the idea of *I Think My Chicken Is a Dinosaur* was born.

For more information and STEAM activities visit kathleenoswald.com or follow on Instagram at @kathleenoswaldwrites.

Printed in the USA
CPSIA information can be obtained
at www.ICGtesting.com
LVHW070551070224
771185LV00012B/302